The World Wide Wood Series

This Book:
Noah's Adventure

First published in paperback by
Michael Terence Publishing in 2023
www.mtp.agency

ISBN 9781800944978

Michael Terence
Publishing

The World Wide Wood

Book 1

NOAH'S ADVENTURE

MIKE RYMARZ

To Karen, Sullivan and Zoe.

Chapter 1

"But why do we have to go? It's not fair! All my friends are here." Noah threw his book down and turned his back away from his dad, staring into the corner of his bedroom.

"It's my job, Noah. You know that. But listen, you'll make new friends. You moved up to secondary school and made friends there, so this is just the same thing. It's just that it's going to be in a different part of England."

Noah couldn't explain, but that wasn't the only thing bugging him. He lived in a big city, and they would be moving to the countryside. How boring! He had everything he ever needed in the city, excitement always right around the corner. And now he was going to be living with cows, and fields, and boredom! He shrugged his dad's hand off his shoulder and moved his body, so he was cramped even further into the corner. His dad quickly got the message and left Noah alone, reflecting on how dull his life was going to become.

Two months later, and his biggest fear had

become a reality. They had left their cosy three-bedroomed flat in the centre of the city and had moved to a large, empty house in a small village called Wychley. The new house had five bedrooms, a huge kitchen which his dad loved immediately as he really enjoyed cooking a big Sunday roast dinner, a back garden the size of a small field where his little sister could play, and three rooms downstairs that his mum was looking forward to decorating straight away. His whole family was delighted with the move – but he wasn't. He could only think about all the fun he was missing back home.

He walked into the lounge and stared out of the window at the small lane that curled past their house. He stared vacantly out of the window for three or four minutes and he didn't see a single car. In their old flat, he could sit for three minutes and see six buses, eight vans, two lorries and dozens of cars, each of them on their way to an exciting destination or delivering goods for the local community. All he saw here was a young woman walking her cocker spaniel and an elderly man on his bike. No children running around, no cars ferrying families to funfairs or festivals, no activity at all.

Except for the same person cycling back the other way. And Noah was convinced this time that the old man stared straight at him, slowly smiled, and winked at him!

Noah ducked under the window, kneeling on the grey carpet and hiding from the stranger's eerie gaze. He waited for thirty seconds, breathing so quickly that he had to cover his own mouth in case anyone heard him. He peeked his head over the windowsill, relieved to see that the old man had already gone past.

"Noah, can you come here, please?" his mum called from their new driveway.

He trudged out of the lounge, kicking the carpet as he went. His mum *sounded* happy but any mum calling their fourteen-year-old out to help on moving day wasn't going to be delivering good news! He had almost reached the car when he looked up and saw his mother chatting to someone standing with their back to Noah. He turned round, and Noah could see it was the same old man who had just winked at him!

"Ah, Noah. Come and meet Mr Atlas. He owns the little shop at the end of the village, and he noticed us moving in. He said if you and Josie want to go down to the shop at some point, he'll very kindly give you a 'welcome to Wychley' present. Isn't that nice of him?"

"Yeah, s'pose so. Thanks, Mr Atlas," he added a second later after catching his mum's menacing glare.

"Well, it is a delight to meet you, young Noah. Are you enjoying it here?"

"I, um," Noah didn't want to seem rude, but his parents had always taught him not to lie, "I haven't seen enough yet, but it seems… nice."

"It's probably a big change from what you're used to," the old man said, "but let me tell you something. You don't realise this yet, but Wychley is the gateway to the world. There is a lot more to discover here than you might think."

Noah wasn't certain, but he thought that maybe Mr Atlas winked at him again. He was starting to feel a little strange about this whole unusual encounter, and excused himself to go back inside again, picking up a small cardboard box to show he was helping. He overheard Mr Atlas and his mum finishing their talk.

"A job?" his mum said with a gleeful song to her voice. "I'm sure he'd love a job. I'll talk to him later and ask him to pop down and see you. Thank you ever so much. Bye."

A job! There was no way he was going to get a job. His time was going to be spent searching for fun or signs of life, or trying to work out which buses took him to the nearest big town. It was the start of the summer so the only thing he really wanted to do was know how he could make this nightmare seem a little less painful!

Chapter 2

Two days later, and Noah still wasn't any happier in Wychley. He had carried out an extensive search of the small village and had discovered the following: there was a total of eighty-five houses – he'd counted them all –, one park, a small convenience store selling a selection of home-grown vegetables, milk, cheese and occasionally sweets and chocolate, and Mr Atlas' small shop which he hadn't visited yet. One bus passed through the village every four hours, and if Noah wanted to get anywhere near anything called civilisation, he had to walk for thirty minutes to another larger village where you could get a bus more regularly.

Noah's mum and dad loved living there, however. They kept going on about 'the fresh air', 'the peace and quiet' and 'the much bigger house to grow into'. Josie was equally as happy about their new life, as any eight-year-old girl would be seeing horses around every corner and giggling at a family of ducks waddling across the road to bathe in whatever available water there was on a hot July day. It helped that she had already made friends with another girl her same age, Summer, and the two mums had quickly planned for them to have tea together at the weekend. Josie was also delighted with the prospect of - if she was a good girl - perhaps getting a dog now they had enough room to really look after one.

Everyone was happy – everyone but Noah. He spent a lot of time listening to music and staring out of his bedroom window, hoping he would see something to make him feel excited. His love of music had come from his mum and dad, both of them preferring CDs and vinyl discs to television, although when they did watch TV, it was normally tuned to a music channel. They now had smart devices in their new home, so Noah could listen to any one of ten million songs whenever he wanted.

"Noah, stop moping about and come into the kitchen. You can give me a hand with dinner." His mum tried to include them as much as possible when it came to household chores, hoping they could pull their own weight and help her when they were older. Noah's dad did his fair share, and particularly loved cooking, often surprising them with a spicy chili con carne, home-made pizzas or a particularly tasty chicken in mushroom sauce. Noah hoped that one day he would be as accomplished a cook as either his mum or dad, and loved trying food from all over the world.

"Coming mum," he replied with a sigh. He wasn't really in the mood, but as he wasn't doing anything else, he figured helping out could amuse him for a short time.

"Pass me the ham out of the fridge, would you?"

"Yeah okay. What you makin'?"

"Ham in a cheese sauce and jacket potatoes. But, listen, can you do something for me? We don't have enough mayonnaise, and I need you to pop down to the convenience store." Ready for any chance to do something vaguely different and interesting, he leapt up and started to put on his trainers. "Oh, and while you're at it, you haven't been to see Mr Atlas yet, have you?"

Oh, hang on a second, Noah thought. So that was really it, was it? She actually wanted me to go and see that weird old man and the mayo was just a trick, like parents like to do sometimes.

"No, I haven't. I'll do it next week."

"No, you won't. Come on, just do it today. You're always finding reasons to put things off. Do it after you get the mayonnaise."

Noah knew not to argue with her, so slouched his way out of the door and onto the country lane. He had been lucky in the city to be given a lot of freedom, often catching the bus or tube by himself or with friends – only as long as he had his phone with the *find my phone* app on it, so his parents knew where he was. This little trip through the village was easy compared to some of the journeys he had experienced back home, as he still referred to their old house in the city.

He found the mayonnaise quickly enough in the small shop, choosing the squeezy bottle instead of the jar because it was easier to carry, and then continued to the end of the lane where Mr Atlas' shop was located. It was the last building he came to on the left, before the road bent round to the right, travelling away from Wychley. Behind the shop, there was a small park with an old set of swings and a picnic table, and behind the park there was a small pathway leading further into some woods. As part of his extensive research, Noah had already explored these woods a little, but all he had seen were a couple of small apple trees, a tiny pond and then more trees. If he had been his sister's age, he would have probably loved running around the forest, or wood, or whatever it was called, pretending to play, or to look for treasure. But he was too old for that now. Playing around in woods was what little kids did, not fourteen-year-olds.

A little bell rang as Noah walked into the shop, probably to let Mr Atlas know that someone was there. As he closed the door behind him, he was sure he caught sight of a squirrel racing from behind the counter and through the curtain of coloured beads that hung down from the ceiling. A squirrel! No, there was no way he could have seen a squirrel running through the shop, he thought to himself. Wow, he'd only been in the village for a couple of days and already he was going mad, seeing imaginary animals!

It was a strange shop to have in a small village, he thought. There were maps all around the walls, and the shelves were filled with ornaments, books and music from different countries. It was an explosion of colours, from bright pink flamingos standing in the corner of the shop, to stacks of wooden Russian dolls on the shelves behind the counter. Noah didn't know where to look – there were so many different objects to see, and books to read. There was a huge, shiny globe in the corner of the shop, although over half of it seemed to be missing. He turned around a full 360 degrees to see models of boats next to his shoulders, or planes hanging from the ceiling. He spotted names of books such as 'Native Tribes of the Amazon' or '101 Sights to See in Singapore'. He stopped reading after a while, his brain befuddled, and his eyes going sleepy from the hundreds of different titles.

"See anything you like, young man?" A slow, deep voice startled Noah who whipped his head round.

"Oh, hi, Mr Atlas. I was, um, just looking."

Mr Atlas laughed. "That's okay, Noah. Feel free to have a look round. Do you enjoy travelling?"

"Well, we've been on a few holidays. You know, warm beach holidays like in Spain and France, and I think we might have gone to Greece when I was younger but, well, I haven't really done much travelling. I know quite a lot about the world though," he said, trying to prove he deserved to be in this amazing shop. "I mean, I know loads of capitals and things about countries."

"That's great, Noah. Just great. Have you come in for that 'welcome to Wychley' present I promised?"

Small presents were given to small children, and Noah didn't want to sound too childish. "No, it's okay, you don't have to give me anything. I'm sure Josie will want something, but I'm alright thanks. I just came in because mum said I should."

Mr Atlas busied himself by adding more books to the shelf, needing a small stepstool to reach some of the higher shelves. "Well, whatever the reason, it's nice that you came in. Tell me, if you could travel to any country in the world, where would you like to go?"

Noah had thought about this question before and knew what his answer was straight away. "Peru," he said confidently.

"Peru. That's a strange answer. Is it because you want to see where Paddington came from?"

Noah laughed. Mr Atlas didn't seem so bad after all. "I'm not sure I'd find Paddington, but I'd love to see Macchu Picchu, and the Andes. My dad told me about them, and they sound cool."

Mr Atlas stepped down and stared at Noah. He took his glasses off and rubbed them with the bottom of his shirt. He waited a second or two before staring directly at Noah and saying the words that Noah would never forget.

"Well, Noah, how about if I could help you to see the world?"

Chapter 3

"What do you mean, see the world? Like, with a globe or something? Or maybe on TV?" Noah was a bit confused about what exactly this strange old man was talking about.

Mr Atlas walked round behind the counter, leaning on it so his face was level with Noah's. "This is only a small shop in a small village, but it's an extremely important shop. Have you been into the woods yet?"

"No." Noah was becoming even more confused, and wasn't at all sure what he was supposed to be learning from this conversation.

"In the woods behind the shop, lives some of the most varied, and important wildlife that has ever lived. Only certain people can see it all, however, and it is my responsibility to make sure all the animals and plants survive and grow. There are some groups of people who don't want them all to live, and, over the past fifty years, they have been doing their best to stop me from caring for them. With various helpers over the years, I slowly collected everything I needed, until three years ago when most of what I had was stolen – or rather spirited – away from me. We need to get everything back and I simply can't do it anymore.

"I've been looking for someone like you, Noah. Someone who is brave, clever, and more importantly, someone who has the desire to want to see the world. I have certain, shall we say, abilities, and I could sense from the very first time I saw you that there was something special about you." He stopped talking and laughed. "You look like you've seen a ghost, young man. Is this all so hard to believe?"

"Well, I, er, I don't really understand. What do you mean you have abilities?" Noah was indeed very confused, and he needed Mr Atlas to explain. The old man sighed deeply before putting his arm round Noah's shoulder.

"I think the best thing is for me to show you. Come, come into the woods and you'll see what I mean." Mr Atlas turned the small sign around on the door to show any potential customers that they were now closed, and he turned the key in the lock. Noah had always been told not to go anywhere with strangers, but his mum had already met Mr Atlas, and she was the one who told him to go to the shops in the first place, so it wasn't like he was being naughty, or that she didn't know where he was. Noah was pretty sure he wasn't in any danger, and he was curious about what the old man had to show him. They walked through the rear of the shop and out of the back door. The sunlight hit Noah immediately, forcing him to turn his head away from the intense glare, squinting his eyes and covering his face with his right hand. Once his eyes had adjusted to the bright light, he took in his surroundings.

He struggled to keep up with the shopkeeper as they walked past the disused playground, through the narrow gap in the trees, finally coming out at a large opening. Noah hadn't noticed this before, but there, in front of him, was a neat circle of trees - seven in total - which surrounded a small green area. Next to each tree, was a small path covered with wood chippings, that extended deeper into the dark woods. Noah stood in the centre of the grassy lawn and spun around, trying to see to the end of each of the paths, straining hard to work out where they finished.

"Here we are, Noah," Mr Atlas declared triumphantly, his arms outstretched. "This is the World Wide Wood, and it is your access to every single country in the world. From here, you can travel all over the planet, but only when the wood allows it. Each tree here represents a different country, and each one has its own rules. Some of them…"

"Woah, hang on a minute. What do you mean, every tree represents a different country? And what do you mean I can get to any country in the world? I mean, that's just impossible!" Noah was dumbstruck about what he was hearing, not believing a word coming out of the crazy old man's mouth.

Mr Atlas didn't say anything, but simply smiled. He started walking towards one of the trees and, without turning around, gestured with his hand for Noah to follow him. Noah did as he was instructed, and they headed down the grassy path to the left of that particular tree.

"Start counting, Noah," he said as they passed the first tree, pointing to it, and then to the next one directly behind it. Noah hadn't noticed before, but each of the seven trees hid a long row of other trees, each one the same size as the first tree, all of them in a neat line. Two minutes later, they had reached the end of the line of trees, and Mr Atlas stopped abruptly and faced his young, bug-eyed and totally confused companion. "Well? How many?"

"I counted fifty-four. So what?" Noah replied with a typical teenage shrug of his shoulders.

"And do you know how many countries there are in Africa, Noah?"

"Um, no. Should I?"

Mr Atlas laughed again. "I suppose not. I've been doing this for so long that I forget others don't know some of the things I do. There are fifty-four countries in Africa. And if you walk down another row you'll find fourteen trees, the same number as in Oceania, or Australasia as it is sometimes called, although some even think the name of the continent is Australia, which I don't agree with and… oh, sorry, I'm going off in a different direction. Now, where was I? Oh yes, another line has forty-four trees, which of course is Europe."

"I still don't get it."

"No, Noah. But you will." Mr Atlas started walking back to where they had started, leaving a befuddled Noah to race after him. When they reached the grassy patch, Noah just stood there, scratching his head and looking as bamboozled as ever about the spectacle unfolding all around him. As he had passed the trees once more, he'd heard a strange sound, almost as if the trees were whispering to him, singing soft lullabies as he neared each one. He was so entranced that he hadn't noticed that Mr Atlas had continued walking towards the shop, and Noah feared he would be left behind. He ran to catch up.

"Mr Atlas. Uh, wait a second," he said as they walked through the back door. "Why are you telling me all this? Why does it matter how many trees there are in each row? And what do you mean I can travel anywhere in the world?"

"So many questions, Noah. I knew you were the right person. Here, look at this globe." He indicated the one in the corner that Noah had spotted when he had first entered the shop, and he reached up, slowly removing it from the shelf. He became more serious, his voice instantly changing in tone. "This is the Globe of Life, and I am its keeper. When it is complete, it gives great power to the wood you've just been in. That wood, in turn, gives life to thousands of creatures, plants, flowers and so on, and these animals and wildlife are distributed all over the world. Without the power from the Globe, the wildlife is in danger of becoming extinct, and, if that happens, it could have catastrophic consequences for the entire planet."

He removed his glasses and rubbed his eyes. "If you look carefully, however, you can see that the Globe is incomplete. As I mentioned earlier, there are evil people who want to destroy all the natural things in the world, and they have cast a spell on the Globe, sending over half the pieces to all the countries of the world. This event has been named the Scattering, and I tell you this to save time later. Now, I have the oceans here, and the North Pole is complete, as are parts of Russia, Brazil, Canada, China. I spent the majority of my life finding these pieces and completing the Globe all by myself, but for the past three years I have just been too old to continue the search. When the Scattering happened, I realised I needed to find an apprentice who could take over this vitally important job for me. I used to have a wonderful pair of helpers not too long ago, two young brothers called James and Josh. They were an amazing help to me, but regrettably they moved away from Wychley. And that is where you come in, young Noah."

Noah didn't quite know what to say, and simply stayed silent for about thirty seconds while Mr Atlas carefully replaced the Globe in its resting place. He finally plucked up the courage to ask some questions.

"So, are you telling me you want me to climb inside a tree and travel all over the world trying to find small pieces of a globe? That's impossible! I wouldn't be able to get my passport from my parents, and there is no way they'd let me go."

"Ah, fear not my young quizzical lad. I told you earlier that you could travel anywhere from the trees. Let me explain. When a tree is ready, it will open a door into its trunk. My team are constantly watching the trees to alert us when one is ready. If you step inside, you will be transported thirty seconds later to another tree in a different country. The trees cannot tell you *where* the piece is located, but, during those thirty seconds, you will hear a piece of music which will be a clue to where you will find what you are looking for. The tree will also give you the money you will need for that country, and all the language skills you will need while you are there. You just have to remember this rhyme:

Greet them like a native, and all will be just fine
If your first word isn't right, you'll have a tricky time.

"I will also give you one of the pieces for you to take with you. It will act like a sort of magnet, if you will, and when you are getting close to the missing piece, the one you have with you will glow. The brighter it glows, the closer you are."

"Hang on, let me just understand something. I can travel anywhere in the world with the trees? If it's so easy, why don't you just go yourself?"

"Good question, Noah. The problem is, the trees can be a little mischievous, you see. You never quite know where they are going to drop you. It could be ten metres or five thousand miles away from the piece you are looking for, and you will need all your skill and cunning to reach your destination in time. As I mentioned before, I'm just too old now for all the travelling. It takes its toll on old, weary bones like mine!"

"There's a time limit?" Noah asked with a hint of worry in his voice.

"Well, sort of. Time travelling through the World Wide Wood doesn't work the same way as it does here. The only ways to return home are either through the same tree in which you arrived - but only for the first ten minutes after you've arrived – or by touching both Globe pieces together. That way, you will instantly come back to the patch of grass in the centre of the tree circle that I just showed you. Don't worry, Noah," he said with a chortle, "it's a soft landing!"

"But what do you mean about a time limit?"

"Oh, yes. Well, if you complete your mission and get back here within seven days of leaving, it will seem as though no time has passed, and you will return to the very moment you left. If you take longer than seven days, however, then time will have continued on here in exactly the same way. Now, I'm sure you don't want your parents to be worried about you for all that time, do you?"

"Well, no, of course not, but…"

Noah wasn't able to finish his sentence because, at that point, three cute, grey squirrels came racing through the back door, and jumped up onto the counter. To Noah's amazement, the first one started speaking.

"Francis…" he squeaked, addressing Mr Atlas, "Francis. One's just opened. A door's open. Do you want to try it?"

"Come on, Francis, come on," the other two squirrels squealed in unison.

Mr Atlas turned to Noah who was staring at the three little talking creatures in absolute disbelief. "Well, Noah. Are you ready for your adventures to begin?"

Chapter 4

"Those squirrels are talking! I mean, they're like, talking!" Noah was flustered, and couldn't quite believe his eyes, or rather his ears.

"Don't worry about those squirrels, Noah. We don't have time right now. I need to know if you're ready to go through."

Well, I, um," Noah tore himself away from the sheer ludicrousy of talking woodland creatures, and looked at the bottle of mayonnaise he had just bought. "I need to get this back to my mum."

"Don't worry about that, Noah. Don't forget, it will be like no time has passed. You need to make up your mind, my boy. The door never stays open for very long. I've not been able to journey myself recently, and I've seen many doors open and close. Too many! It's been so frustrating that, for the past few years, whenever a door has been ready, I haven't been able to take advantage of it, so it would be a shame to miss this one. I don't mean to pressure you, Noah, but I need your help. *We* need your help. In fact, *the whole world* really needs your help, before it gets too late." He reached up to the Globe, removed one piece, and marched out of the back door, followed swiftly by the squirrels. Noah, reeling from everything he'd just learned, but feeling it only right to at least see what an open tree-door looked like, ran after him.

In less than a minute, they were back in the middle of the grassy patch, and the squirrels were now leading the way. They headed down the row of trees Noah remembered as having represented Europe, and stopped when they reached the tenth tree. Unlike all the others, this particular tree had an opening, large enough for Noah to fit through. A section of the trunk had lifted up like a giant cat-flap, allowing access into the darkness of the tree's interior. Noah peered in, but could hardly see a thing.

"It's now or never, Noah. You have to make your mind up. Do you want to help me rebuild the Globe? If so, this is the first step." Mr Atlas leaned back and held his right arm out, guiding Noah towards the open door.

Noah had wanted to find excitement and adventure in this sleepy little village, but this was beyond all his wildest dreams. He had thought of maybe catching a train into the city centre, or jumping on the bus like he used to, but this excitement was on a completely different scale. Mind you, would he always regret not doing this? If Mr Atlas was right, this was his chance to see the world!

"OK," he said with a little hesitation. "I'll do it."

Mr Atlas gave him a huge, beaming smile, obviously seeing how nervous Noah was. "Attaboy, Noah. I knew I could count on you. Now, take this piece, and in you go." He pressed the piece of the Globe into Noah's hand, who firmly shoved it into his jeans pocket. "Just remember that you have everything you'll need in the tree." He nudged Noah forward, who tentatively stepped into the middle of the tree trunk.

As soon as he was in, the door closed behind him, and a light appeared above his head. A piece of music suddenly started playing, that Noah recognised immediately from his dad's music collection.

Lean on Me
When you're not strong
And I'll be your friend
I'll help you carry on…
For it won't be long
Till I'm gonna need somebody to lean on

The song continued, and Noah hummed along to it, wondering why he was hearing it and what the tune meant. To his right, there was a small shelf, and on it was a pile of money, bound together by a small piece of tape. On the tape was written the word 'Euros'.

"OK," he said to himself, "that narrows it down a little." He racked his brain trying to remember which countries used euros. He recognised the notes from a family trip to France, and he knew that Germany, Spain, Italy, Greece, and a few other countries used euros, so hoped that wherever he was going, he might know something about the country. Facing the area where he had walked in, he saw the word *'Ciao'* etched above the door. But, before he really had time to take it all in, the music stopped, and a door swung open, this time more of a fairly normal, traditional looking door that he could walk through without crouching.

He was met with dazzling sunshine, momentarily blinding him. He had to blink a few times before stepping out. In front of him, the dark wood had disappeared, and there was a small bush, behind which was a brown, wooden bench and a green bin. He looked around and couldn't see anyone, and felt relieved that no-one had noticed him just step out of a tree! He spied a small opening in the bush and walked through, finding himself on a gravel path. He turned his body from side to side, and saw a few more benches, a small playground and a stone wall. Noah walked over to it, feeling hot and sweaty in the intense heat. Beyond the wall, he could just about make out a mass of water with bridges as far as he could see, a few buildings on the other side, and some strange boats in the water.

"Excuse me," he said to a woman who was watching a young child on the swings, "where am I?"

"Mi scusi, non capisco," she said in a foreign language.

"Ah, man. How am I supposed to understand people?" he muttered to himself. "I've got no idea where I am, and I can't even ask for anyone's help." He sat down on one of the benches, and put his head in his hands. He was so angry. Angry and disappointed. Why on earth did he agree to do this? That was it, he thought, this adventure was finished! He was going to go back through the tree he had just arrived in without achieving a single thing. He stood up and walked back through the gap in the bush, looking around to make sure no-one was watching him. He ran his fingers around the edge of the tree and found a small slit in the tree where the door sat. He levered the door open a tiny bit and slid inside, closing it firmly behind him. No more than five seconds passed this time before the door swung open again, and standing in front of him were Mr Atlas and the three squirrels.

Chapter 5

"Ah, there you are, Noah? Did you find it already?" Mr Atlas asked, his hands on his hips.

"No, and I'm not doing any more of these stupid adventures. How can I go anywhere if I don't speak the language? It's stupid." Noah pushed past Mr Atlas and stomped towards the shop.

"Wait, Noah. One second. Have you already forgotten all the rules?" Mr Atlas wasn't chasing after him, but just stayed rooted to the spot.

"What do you mean, rules?" Noah said over his shoulder as he continued marching away.

"Don't you remember?

Greet them like a native, and all will be just fine
If your first word isn't right, you'll have a tricky time.

"Everything you need is there for you, don't forget that. You just have to make sure you use whatever word the tree gives you first. Now, I know it's probably a bit scary, but why don't you give it one more chance?"

Noah stopped walking and turned around. Of course, what an idiot he had been. He needed to say *'Ciao'* before saying anything else. He wasn't quite sure *why* that would help, but he had to trust that, somehow, this magic that allowed him to travel anywhere in the world would help him with his language problems.

"Maybe I'll give it one more go," he said slowly, ambling back to the tree Mr Atlas was standing next to.

"That's a good lad. Now, just remember, say whatever is written over the door, and you'll be fine. Do you know where you were? No, wait, don't tell me. You have to come up with all the answers yourself, or the task will be a lot more difficult. Rules are rules after all."

Noah was getting tired of hearing about rules, but he nodded his agreement. He stepped back into the tree, turning round immediately to see the door swing shut, and the light come back on. There was a new pile of bank notes on the shelf, and Noah felt in his pocket to see where the other pile was. It had gone. Disappeared. He grabbed the new pile, and shoved them deep into his pocket, wondering what had happened to the other money. The same music played as before -

the thirty seconds feeling like five minutes – and, finally, he was back out in the same park he had been in before. He followed the same routine as before, ensuring no-one was watching him, and then walked over to the same woman he had spoken to the first time.

"Ciao!" he said confidently.

"Ciao. Are you okay?" she said.

He could understand her! "I'm good, thanks." From the look on her face, she could understand him too.

Greet them like a native, and all will be just fine

"Um, I just wondered where we are."

The lady had a perplexed look on her face and chuckled. "Why, we are in the *Giordini Popodopoli* of course." She must have thought Noah crazy!

"Oh, yes, and, um, which city is that in?"

The lady had that 'he's mad' look again on her face. "We're in Venice. The most magnificent city in Italy!" She saw her daughter in trouble on the swing. "Please excuse me."

Italy. They were in Italy. And more

specifically, they were in Venice. Noah had heard about Venice, the city built on water. He left the park with a spring in his step, and started to wander around the streets. Everywhere he looked there was water. One main river ran through the centre of the city, which he discovered from the tourist boards placed all around was called the Grand Canal, and, after that, there were many other small rivers, or canals, or streams, all connected to each other. He quickly lost count of the number of bridges he walked over or could see in the distance. It was one climb after another, some bridges very fancy looking and others just a plain block of stone or concrete.

And it wasn't just the bridges he lost count of, but also the boats. There were motor boats, thin boats of all different colours, wider craft with colourful canopies, and a huge number of long, thin boats with curved ends. Noah understood these were called *gondolas*, and there was a man or woman in control of each gondola, dressed in a black and white stripy t-shirt with a red sash around his or her waist, and a straw summer hat. These drivers – was that the name, Noah thought? – were each pushing a long, brown pole into the water until Noah could barely see it, and then at the last moment pulling it up again so they could perform the same action over and over again. This helped to move the boat, or rather gondola, forward while two tourists sat back and enjoyed the scenery. Noah was fascinated watching them, and had to remind himself he was on a mission.

"This place is amazing," he said to himself as he crossed yet another bridge. "But where is the missing Globe piece?" He took the piece Mr Atlas had given him out of his pocket and looked at it. Nothing was glowing. Not even a tiny hint of light from it. "So, not around here then. Hmm, I wonder where I need to go."

He was finding it hard to concentrate, as the main sound he could hear was his own stomach rumbling. Maybe travelling thousands of miles away can make you hungry, he thought, and set about trying to find some food. He couldn't remember what Italian people ate a lot of until he saw a few signs. Ice-cream, although here it was called *gelato*. Pasta. Pizza. Of course, he thought. Pizza. And he just loved pizza. Absolutely adored it. He found a small window in a building on a corner, a green stripy awning hanging from the side of the building providing him with some welcome shade. He looked in at the tantalising slices teasing him, and slowly fished out a single note from his pocket, not wanting to show too much of his money to anyone watching him. He saw a slice marked *Quatro Stagioni*, which he instinctively understood as *Four Seasons*, and he chose that one. He wanted a drink as well, so picked out a *succo di mela*, as he loved apple juice. The food and juice cost him fifteen euros, which seemed quite a lot, but then he had a whole pile of money, so he thought, why not?

Noah looked for a small bench to sit on, but couldn't find one anywhere. It was almost as if they didn't want anyone just sitting around, making the city look untidy. He carefully cradled the juice carton under his arm, while he munched on the pizza as he strolled along.

Noah was concentrating so much on holding the pizza and not dropping the juice carton, however, that his focus wasn't on where he was walking. The sights around him were so new, and spectacular, that his attention was on the clear blue sky, staring into the distance, and constantly craning his neck for a better view. He found himself ambling through a maze of white stone and red brick roads, with imposing buildings looming over him.

Twisting and turning for a better view, he let go of the juice carton, which slid out from under his arm.

Instinctively, he reached for the drink, inadvertently losing control of the pizza, which fell to the ground with a splat.

At that exact moment, a young couple walked past, hand-in-hand, gazing into each other's eyes. The woman slipped on the pizza, her right foot flying up in the air. She wobbled precariously on her left leg, lost grip of her boyfriend's hand and fell backwards, landing with a resounding splash in the canal.

Noah stared in shock as the angry man heaved his girlfriend out of the canal and then pointed accusingly at Noah.

"Oi! I'm going to get you! Come here!"

Noah ran, not wanting to see what would happen if the man did 'get him', and darted through the streets. He shouldered his way past confused tourists, careful not to knock any more into the water!

"Come here!" he heard, from the angry Italian who was gaining on him. Noah turned left down one street, ran over a bridge, turned right into a second street, until he realised with a sinking heart that he had reached a dead-end. There was water to the right and left of him, locked doors ahead, and the only way out was in the direction he had just come from. A way that was blocked by a very angry boyfriend.

"You're in trouble now," the man said, as he advanced towards Noah. The young traveler took a couple of paces back, wondering how on earth he was going to escape. He flicked his head to the left, and saw a wide canal, too wide for him to jump over. He turned to his right and saw two gondolas creep into view from opposite directions. They were about to cross and Noah saw his chance.

He sprang onto the first gondola before the angry boyfriend had a chance to grab him. Startled passengers cried out, but Noah didn't stop to explain. He carried on running, and, in two quick strides, leaped onto the second gondola, now level with the first. Ignoring the startled passengers' shouts, and seeing that he was close enough to the other side, he held his breath and jumped.

Safely back on dry land, he turned around just in time to see the man try to follow him. The Italian tripped as he jumped, missing the first gondola, and landing straight in the water. Noah sped away, safe in the knowledge that the chase was over.

Unnerved by the incident with the angry boyfriend, Noah continued to walk around the city, checking every now and again that no-one was following him, until he came across a huge cathedral at the end of a large square. There were hundreds of people walking around, bumping into each other and taking photos of the cathedral, or Saint Mark's Basilica as he learned from the signs in front.

"This must be it," he said breathlessly. It was a huge building, one of the biggest in the city, so this must be where the piece was hidden. He hurriedly put his hand in his pocket and felt for the Globe piece, hoping he could feel some kind of warmth or heat coming from it. He pulled it out and stared at it, excited to see what a shiny Globe piece would look like.

Chapter 6

Nothing. Once again. Not even a faint glow. Noah was really starting to get worried now. "If it's not here, then where could it be?" he asked himself, his voice rising to a small panic. He suddenly clicked his fingers. "Of course, it doesn't just have to be in Venice, it could be anywhere in Italy. And it's probably going to be in Rome. That's the capital, and all the big monuments are in Rome. So, that's it. I need to go to Rome." He realised he was talking quite loudly, but no-one near him seemed to take any notice of what he was saying.

He started to walk towards a large board that showed a map of the city, hoping he could find the way to the central train station. The board was a maze of canals, rivers and streets, and it took him a moment to work out where he was, despite a large red arrow pointing to St Mark's square with a sign saying 'YOU ARE HERE'! He traced his way to the railway station, the *Stazione di Venezia Saint Lucia,* and saw that it was almost a straight line north. Well, it would have been if he had been a bird.

It didn't take him long to weave his way between all the old buildings, over the stone bridges and past all the tourists, busy taking photos of the wonderful sights. Noah didn't have time to appreciate the beauty of the city anymore, as he was focused on reaching the train station as quickly as possible. He seemed to be moving faster than he normally did at home, although he figured this was probably because he was so excited. It took him less than ten minutes and, before he knew it, he was at the entrance to the train station. And what a spectacular entrance it was! The station was a very wide, white building, with steps stretching across the entire front, leading up to the dark, glass doors.

As soon as Noah walked in, he felt the cool blast from the air conditioning, a great relief from the intense heat outside. He hadn't been fully aware of how hot it really was until he felt the contrast from the cool interior of the train station, but he was glad of the difference. He soon found the ticket office, and walked up to the counter.

"A single child's ticket to Rome, please," he said, understanding that there was no point asking for a return.

"Is it for you, mate?" the young man behind the counter said.

"Er, yeah, of course." Noah was hoping there was no rule about travelling alone as a child in Italy.

"Well then, you need an adult's ticket, unless you look much older than you are." He printed off a ticket before Noah had a chance to argue, and handed it to him, asking for ninety-five euros in return. Noah wandered off in bemusement, until he stumbled across some glass panels that were so dark, they acted like mirrors. He couldn't believe what he was seeing. The person staring back at him *looked* like him, but he was older, with a stronger jaw, a small amount of hair under his chin, and a few more muscles in his chest, arms and shoulders.

"Wow!" he exclaimed. "I'm hench! This is sick!" He stood there, flexing his muscles and admiring how old and mature he looked. He had no idea how this had happened, but then he was finding it tough to explain anything that had happened in the past five hours!

Accepting this amazing, but very welcome, transformation, he looked up at the huge screens with all the train times and platform information. Florence, platform three, Naples, platform one, Trieste, platform six. Rome – there it was, platform four. He scanned the entire station to see where he had to go, and how long before he had to wait. Blimey, he only had eight minutes until the train left, he thought, as he started to break into a panicked run. The train was due to leave at twenty to six, and it was already after half-past five, and there were quite a few people now rushing to catch their own trains.

He easily found the entrance that led to platforms three and four, and found himself being carried along in a wave of passengers, some going to the right and some to the left. There was such a mass of people that he was spun around a couple of times in the hustle and bustle of everything going on, until he found himself at last stood in front of the train, an open door inviting him in. He jumped on board and slumped into a seat, exhausted from the rush of trying to catch his train, just in time as it started to pull out of the station. We're on our way, he thought with relief.

He aimlessly stared out of the window catching sight of the boards with the number of the platform on them as they passed at an increasing pace. The problem was, it wasn't the number four as expected on those boards, but it was the number three he kept seeing!

Chapter 7

"Ah, no, I'm on the wrong train!" he shouted, the other passengers looking up at what this mad, English-speaking child, or rather, man, was yelling about. He leaned forward, and tapped the person in the seat just the other side of the gangway.

"Excuse me, which train is this?"

The passenger turned to him with a confused look on his face. "It's the 5:38 to Florence."

He was going to Florence, not Rome! And he had no idea where Florence was. In the rush, he must have jumped, or been pushed, on to the wrong train, and now here he was, on his way to somewhere which could be hundreds of miles away from where he needed to be. This day was going from bad to worse.

He stood up and started to make his way through the train carriage, praying that he would be able to come up with a solution for his current problem. He passed families, business people, young men with headphones on, listening to whatever the latest Italian hit song was at the time, and elderly couples, obviously going home after a busy day sightseeing. He needed to find a map of the country to see how far away he was going to be. Florence. It sounded nice, but he was pretty sure he had never heard of it before.

He noticed that the carriages were nicer than the trains he'd been on in England. They were clean, with emerald green fabric on the seats, each one with thin, red, vertical stripes running through them. There was ample space for people's cases and bags, either over head or in metal racks at each end where the seats stopped. The aisles were quite wide as well, not like the thin gangways he was used to, where he had to squeeze past anyone coming the other way. The automatic doors opened with a quiet 'whoosh', the repetitive nature of it and the gentle rocking of the train from side to side making Noah feel extremely tired, although there was no danger of falling asleep if he continued walking.

He needed to work out where they were going; he had no idea if this train journey was going to last ten minutes or ten hours! He eventually came to the buffet car, the usual rows of seats in other carriages replaced with high, steel tables dotted around where a few passengers were standing and drinking *espressos* - strong, small and very rich Italian coffees - and munching on snacks. There was a counter running almost the whole length of the room which served tasty looking food such as sandwiches, biscuits, chocolate and drinks. Noah wasn't hungry, or even thirsty, after his pizza and juice from earlier, but started to daydream about which of the tasty meals he would choose if he was going to be on the train for a long time. He was snapped out of his wandering thoughts when he saw something that just might possibly change his luck. By the entrance to the buffet carriage, there was a metal, rotating stand with dozens of leaflets, maps, and information about all the sights to see and places to visit in Italy. They were in many different languages – not that Italian was posing him any problems thanks to the magic of the tree – and he found the English versions in amongst the French, German and Spanish ones.

The first leaflet he picked up showed a map of the whole country with funny cartoons depicting the different sights to see. Italy was a strange shape, a little like a boot that was kicking a ball at the bottom, the ball being an island which he saw was called Sicily. Venice, the city he had just left, was all the way at the top on the right-hand side of the country, on the coast of a small area of water called the Adriatic Sea. To the west of Venice, indicated on the cartoon map by bridges and gondolas, he traced his hand over to Verona, Milan and then Turin, and moving directly south – a long way south – he found Rome, with a drawing of a huge amphitheatre next to it. Just below that was Naples – finally another name he recognised – but underneath that, the names of the towns and cities were all completely unknown to him.

He searched the map until he located Florence, probably two-thirds of the way to Rome. Phew, he thought, at least he was travelling in roughly the right direction. It shouldn't be that difficult to find a train from Florence that would go on to Rome, he reasoned, and it wasn't miles out of the way of his final destination. Noah's mood picked up with this revelation, and he felt like he wanted to celebrate. He was about to replace the map in the metal stand when two incredibly important things happened. Firstly, another leaflet caught his eye, and secondly, he heard some familiar music start to play over the tannoy.

The music was a song his dad used to play from the seventies or eighties, and it was exactly the same piece of music he had heard in the tree. It all came flooding back to him. Of course, the music! He was supposed to listen to the music in the tree to help him work out where the missing piece of the Globe was. In all the excitement of everything else, he had totally forgotten about that vital bit of information, and he had foolishly jumped onto a train to go to Rome, simply because that was the capital of Italy. He slapped his forehead with the palm of his hand, silently berating himself for being such an idiot.

Lean on Me
When you're not strong
And I'll be your friend
I'll help you carry on…
For it won't be long
Till I'm gonna need somebody to lean on

'Lean on Me'. He couldn't remember who sang it, but his mum and dad used to play it a lot on car journeys, and in the kitchen when they were cooking up Sunday roast. Despite excitement coursing through his body, he stopped for a second, the sudden memories of his parents making him wish he was back home with them and not travelling through a foreign land. He quickly shook that thought of his head, realising the only way he was going to get back to them was to find the missing piece as quickly as he could. He turned his attention back to the leaflet that had caught his eye. On the front cover of the leaflet was a picture of a tall, white tower, with hundreds of vertical columns on every floor. But the strange thing was, the columns were not quite vertical because they were at an angle. And the reason they were at an angle was because the entire tower was leaning to one side. Excited thoughts raced through his mind, his palms clammy as he removed the leaflet, revealing the name of the tower at the bottom – the Leaning Tower of Pisa!

Chapter 8

The Leaning Tower of Pisa. Lean on Me. They *have* to be connected, he thought. Surely he was right with this. He popped the leaflet in his pocket, and spent the next five minutes rifling through the others nestled in the stand. The one about Rome showed a picture of the Colosseum (the huge amphitheatre he had seen on the first map), the Spanish steps and the Trevi Fountain. He picked up one about Milan, which enthused about the spectacular San Siro stadium, and read other booklets about the Giant's Fountain and Ovo in Naples, and the ruins of Pompeii nearby. There was even a little pamphlet about St Peter's Basilica in the Vatican City, which was apparently a country in the centre of Rome. Bit strange that, he thought, but he put it to the back of his mind. His focus was solely on whether there was anything else in Italy which could possibly lean, or have some kind of link to the song.

He saw a couple of people about his parent's age, eating a sandwich and drinking two fizzy drinks. They reminded him so much of his parents, the man going slightly bald and with the same kind of pastel-coloured jumpers his dad wore, and the woman with her short, brown hair which she flicked away from her eyes in the same way his mum did. He had to remind himself that they weren't his parents, and that he was still alone here. He walked over to them and addressed them in the Italian that he knew so well by now.

"Excuse me, do you know any other monuments in Italy apart from the tower in Pisa that lean, or have anything to do with leaning?"

"Sorry, mate, don't speak any Italian," the man said, holding his hands in the air as if he was either surrendering or apologizing.

"Oh, you're English," Noah replied, asking the question again, but this time in English.

"Yeah, we're English, and no," he said, confirming with his wife, "we don't know any others. That's the most famous though. Are you going to see it?"

"Definitely," said Noah, feeling more and more convinced that he was on the right track. "Do you think I'll be able to get another train from Florence to Pisa?"

"I'm sure you will," said the woman in a comforting manner, similar to how Noah's mother would often speak to him, "but I'm afraid there probably won't be any this late in the day. Are you staying in Florence tonight?"

Noah hadn't even thought about that. If he couldn't catch another train today, he would need to stay in Florence overnight, and then travel to Pisa the next day, and he didn't have a clue where to stay. He explained to the couple that he didn't know the area very well, and asked if they had any suggestions.

"As it happens, we know of a good, cheap hotel chain that you can stay in. Here," the man said, reaching out for the leaflet about Pisa, "let me give you the address of the best hotel. It's only about forty euros for the night, and they give you breakfast as well."

The man took a pen out of his pocket, checked his smartphone for about thirty seconds, and then wrote down the name of a hotel, and the street it was on.

"Our train should arrive about nine o'clock tonight. If you have time when you arrive, you should check out some of the sights," the woman said enthusiastically. "It's a beautiful city. There is the Ponte Vecchio, a bridge which crosses the river Arno, there is a fantastic cathedral, and then of course you have the statue of David by Michelangelo. Although, thinking about it, the real one is in the Accademia Gallery, so you might have to settle for one of the copies." She moved away from the table and looked at the stand with all the pamphlets. "Here you go," she said, passing him one of the leaflets. "Take a look at some of these."

Noah thanked them for all the information, and returned to his original seat. He was feeling a mixture of excitement, nervousness and anticipation about what might lie ahead on the next step of his journey. He glanced at the digital clock on the wall and then at the arrival times displayed on the flashing screen over the doors to work out when the train would arrive. Probably another two hours or so before he got to Florence, where he would be one step closer to finding what he needed to. He flicked through the leaflets the kind woman had given him, not too sure if he wanted to take her up on her recommendation to see yet another bridge, no matter how interesting and busy it looked! He also wasn't too keen on seeing the statue of David, which turned out to be a naked man from hundreds of years ago. Maybe he'd wander around seeing what else the city had to offer, he guessed with a smile.

The rest of the journey passed fairly quickly, the summer evening allowing him to see easily out of the train window as it sped to its destination, the ever-changing scenery keeping him amused. Before he knew it, they were pulling into the *Santa Maria Novella* train station, and everyone was picking up their bags, ready to disembark. Noah didn't have any baggage with him, of course, so he was one of the first off the train. He ambled down the platform towards the exit, glad that the ticket barrier was open and that there didn't seem to be any staff around. He looked at his incorrect ticket marked 'Rome' and guessed he would have experienced a bit of difficulty if he'd have tried to use that to get through. Maybe luck was on his side for once, he thought with a smile.

He looked up at the big screen with all the train information. He wanted to see what time the trains would leave in the morning, and how long it would take him to get to Pisa. He couldn't quite believe what he was seeing. He looked at the digital clock, then at a large, round, golden traditional clock suspended from the centre of the station, and then back up at the screen, and he then repeated the whole routine again, just in case he'd missed anything. He hadn't. There was a train leaving for Pisa in the next hour.

Chapter 9

He could get to his destination by midnight, he thought. And be in touching distance of the Globe piece he needed to get home. He could feel the rest of the passengers brushing past him as he just stood there, dumbstruck by what he was seeing. He nervously felt the pocket of his jeans to make sure the piece was still there, safely tucked away. He pulled it out a fraction of an inch just on the off chance he had made a small mistake. The piece wasn't glowing, but he was sure it was a tiny bit lighter than it had been earlier in the day. Maybe it was just his mind playing tricks on him, and convincing him that he was going in the right direction. Knowing the piece was safe, he started to think more clearly. If he did leave now, he'd arrive in Pisa late at night, and he would be in a completely foreign city with no idea of where to go. If he stayed in Florence, he could go to the hotel that the nice couple told him about, see one or two sights, and then leave on an early train in the morning. He thought long and hard about it, and came to a decision. When would he next be in Florence, with the opportunity to explore and have another adventure such as this? His dad had always said that when he was older, he would regret what he didn't do, and he didn't want to grow up with any regrets. He decided to take some time and explore the city, and move on to Pisa in the morning. Mr Atlas had said that he had seven days, after all.

He took a mental note of the times the trains departed the following day, and left the station to the welcome of the cool, July evening air. The sun had started to fade, leaving long shadows in some places and areas of darkness in others, but that was to be expected at this time of the night. It still wasn't cold enough for a jacket though, something he was glad of seeing as he hadn't brought one with him. He immediately walked into a large square or *piazza*, with groups of tables all around where diners sat finishing their dinner and drinking glasses of what looked like wine and brandy. There was a murmur of animated conversation, laughter filling the Florentine air mixed with the clinking of glasses. Noah felt a tiny pang of jealousy that he had no-one to share this with, but shook that feeling away when he imagined telling Mr Atlas about his adventures.

There was a cathedral at the back of the

piazza, something which he was becoming used to seeing already in Italy. It must be a very religious country, he guessed, particularly as he'd noticed that a number of houses and buildings in Venice and Florence had crucifixes over the doors. He turned right and headed towards the river, passing small stalls of vendors selling Italian football kits and motor racing hats with the name Ferrari emblazoned all over. There were t-shirts aplenty, most of them with an image of the nude statue – David, he remembered – or with funny slogans all over them about loving *gelato* or Star Wars memes.

Noah smiled as he waited at the roadside, small motorbikes called Vespas nipping in front of other cars trying to find parking spaces. There was a high, stone wall on the riverbank, a totally different experience to Venice where he could have literally leant over and fallen into the water if he had wanted to – which of course is what had happened to the lovey-dovey couple! He looked left and right as he neared the wall, seeing only one bridge either way. His view was blocked to the right by a strange looking bridge, which had what looked like houses built on top and a roof running the whole width of the river. He pulled out the leaflet from the train and saw that this must be the famous *Ponte Vecchio*. Interesting, he admitted, and different from the hundreds of bridges he saw in Venice, but it was only a bridge after all, he thought. Nothing to really write home about.

He stepped out into the road, looking right first as he had always been taught to by his parents.

"BEEEEEP!"

He leaped back from the road, realising only at the last second, as a Vespa whizzed past him, that he should have looked left, as the cars and motorbikes travelled on the other side of the road here. Noah breathed a huge sigh of relief that the Vespa rider had been quick enough to toot his horn and swerve past him. He decided to walk on the path, keeping the river on his left, weaving his way in between small stone columns, under arches, past more cafés and restaurants. The world was still so much more alive here than it would be at this time of night back home, where everyone would be curled up in front of the television with mugs of hot chocolate. In fact, he thought, his sister would already be in bed by this time, and he wouldn't be too far behind. He carried on walking, aimlessly, not caring which street he turned down, or which piazza he ended up in, but always aware of potential danger around him.

Before he realised it, he found himself staring at a hotel name he recognised. He compared it to the one written on the leaflet, and realised that maybe his wandering hadn't been quite so aimless. He'd never had to book a hotel room before, and wasn't exactly sure how to do it. He stood outside for a minute and thought about what he had heard his parents say when they booked into hotels. Number of rooms? One. Number of nights? One. Breakfast the next day?

Oh, yeah, most definitely. He walked in, gave all the information, and they insisted that he paid the forty-three euros straight away, which he was happy to do.

Luckily, it all went smoothly and within a few minutes he was safe and sound in a hotel room. He scanned the room and saw a bed, a small chair, a table with a pencil and notepad with the name of the hotel on it, and of course a small bathroom. It was tiny, and the road out front was full of busy traffic, but Noah felt like a king because it was all his! It was the first time he'd stayed in a hotel by himself, and he was in control! The air conditioning was broken, so he opened the window nice and wide, and admired the view from his second-floor bedroom.

If he hadn't been so tired, he would have kicked off his shoes and watched television for hours, but he was so exhausted that he nestled down on the bed, and couldn't resist the urge to close his eyes.

He woke with a start, and could hear voices shouting from downstairs. The room was in total darkness. Noah shot out of bed, and fumbled around for his clothes and shoes, forcing them on just as the door was flung open.

"Get up, get up," a man in a dark blue uniform yelled at him. "Downstairs, now!"

He grabbed Noah by the arm, yanking him out into the corridor, and pushed him downstairs, along with a bunch of other startled and half-asleep hotel guests.

"What's going on?" Noah asked, but he was met with stony silence. He heard something about illegal immigrant checks, but that didn't mean anything to him.

They were all marched outside, where there were bright, flashing lights coming from three police cars, and a growing crowd. Noah was pushed up against a wall, while police officers walked up and down. Noah saw that it was not even five o'clock in the morning, although delivery vans and lorries were already bustling around, preparing for another busy day.

"Your papers," one of the police officers said.

Noah quickly realised this was going to be a problem.

"My what?" he replied, stalling for time.

"Your papers. Or passport. I need to see them," the police woman said.

"Oh, they're in my room. Would you like me to get them?" Noah said, racking his brains, trying to devise a plan. The female officer signaled to a second policeman, who accompanied Noah back up the stairs to the second floor.

As they walked the last few metres towards the door, a plan started to formulate in Noah's mind. He slowed his pace just enough for the policeman to get close to him, and then stopped abruptly. The policeman walked into Noah, who spun round and shoved him as hard as he could. The policeman fell backwards, allowing Noah enough time to race into his room. He scooped up his bundle of money, and ran towards the open window. The policeman was back on his feet and charging towards him, but Noah was already half-way out of the window. He took a deep breath, and jumped.

Chapter 10

His timing was perfect, and he landed directly on top of a lorry, clinging on as the lorry driver swerved a fraction to the left. Fortunately, the lorry continued on its course, and the angry, thundering shouts from Noah's bedroom window became fainter. Noah flattened himself against the lorry's roof, and stayed in that position until they were far enough away from the hotel that he felt sure he was out of danger. At a set of traffic lights, he managed to slide down the back of the lorry, jumping off just as the unsuspecting getaway driver pulled off.

Doubled over, and breathing heavily from the daring escape, he hid behind some pillars. It took Noah a good five minutes to fully regain his composure. He had never experienced anything like that before, and was hoping the police wouldn't come looking for him. He peered out from his hiding place before feeling confident that he could continue his adventure.

He needed to do two things; firstly, get breakfast, and secondly, find the train station. He made his way to a small café where he was greeted by an array of delicious looking food, a welcome sight for his rumbling stomach. There were some pastries called *Fette Biscottate*, and *Sacottino*, but he settled for some Italian bread and jam, followed by a *Ciambella*, which he understood to be an Italian doughnut. To drink, he chose a hot chocolate and a fruit juice, and wolfed it all down in the space of five minutes. After his adventures of the past thirty minutes, he wasn't sure he had ever had such a tasty breakfast, not that he would ever be able to tell his parents that!

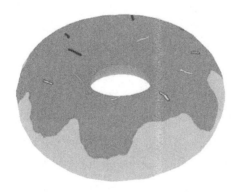

He left the café, and eventually found the train station, ducking into side streets to hide every time he saw a police car zoom past. As he had seen the night before, there was a train every hour to Pisa, and each one took just over an hour to get there. He checked the big clock and saw that the next train would be leaving in fifteen minutes. Perfect! Two minutes, and ten euros, later, he had a ticket for the train on platform five, which he found easily. There were fewer people here than there had been in Venice the day before, and he took extra care to get on the right train this time. He really didn't fancy ending up hundreds of miles away, certainly not now that he was convinced that he had found the right monument.

The journey was a breeze this time – he was becoming quite the expert at train travel. He couldn't stop smiling the whole way there, exceedingly happy that the police were no longer chasing him. Just over one hour later, at 10:44, the train pulled into *Pisa Centrale,* the central train station in Pisa.

As soon as Noah arrived, he took the Globe piece out of his pocket. He stared at it in astonishment as a faint light shone from it. It wasn't a bright light - not yet - but he could see that it was glowing. That could only mean one thing. He was definitely in the right place!

The other passengers stared at Noah in amusement as he made a 'whooping' noise, before jogging down the platform, inserting his ticket into the machine at the end of the platform where the gates opened to allow him through. He easily located the entrance, or rather the exit, and walked through the concourse, turning back to pick up a free map of the city, and finally out to another gorgeous, sunny day.

He opened the map and laid it out on a small stone bench in front of the station entrance, just by a small patch of grass with a pretty fountain only a couple of metres away. He easily found the *Torre de Pisa* which was only a short walk, maybe twenty to twenty-five minutes. He started off at a fairly steady pace, his heart wanting him to run at breakneck speed, but his head telling him to calm down, and not tire himself out. He had no idea how difficult it was going to be to find the piece once he got there, and he wanted to make sure he had enough energy for that.

Within ten minutes, after walking down a lot of dirty streets with roadworks all over the place, he came to a bridge to cross a river. "Is this all Italy has?" he mumbled, with a smile. "Rivers and bridges." However, after the beauty of Venice and the excitement of Florence, this was hands down the most boring river and bridge he had ever seen in his whole life. He stopped half-way across and looked down, just to see if there was anything more interesting happening on the water. There wasn't. As he was straightening up though, he walked backwards and bumped into a man who was jogging along the path. The force of the bump sent Noah lurching forward, and he slammed into the metal barrier preventing him from falling headfirst into the river Arno – the same river he had seen in Florence!

The jogger shouted some furious words which Noah understood, but wished he hadn't, and Noah thanked his lucky stars that the barrier had been there to stop him.

"Phew," he said, brushing his hand across his forehead. "No more messing around, Noah," he told himself, and set off on what he hoped would be the final leg of his journey. After the scenic beauty of the last two cities he had visited, Pisa seemed a bit more down to earth and 'real' Italian – not that Noah had the first clue what real Italy looked like, he guessed. There didn't seem to be as many tourists here, or at least not where he was walking, and he kept his hand tightly encircled around the vital piece in his pocket. He strolled past a high, stone wall on his right which, when he peeked through the gates, he could see housed some kind of public gardens. He had been expecting to see a huge tower rise up above the buildings and shout to him 'here I am', but he couldn't see anything.

He followed the map and saw that he was only a couple of minutes away. He pulled the piece out of his pocket, and it was brighter than before. Much brighter.

"Getting closer," he murmured happily to himself. "Getting closer."

He crossed another small road, and ahead of him was one of those piazzas he had seen in Venice and Florence. There were suddenly a lot more people milling around, some entering or leaving cafés and restaurants, and most of them walking in the same direction he was, cameras in their hands. He walked around a corner and there, in front of him, suddenly appearing out of nowhere, was a fairly large, white tower, leaning over to one side. Maybe not as tall as he would have expected, and definitely not that wide, but impressive all the same. There was a crowd of tourists standing in front of it, with friends or family taking photos of them with their hands positioned perfectly, so it looked like they were trying to straighten it or stop it from completely falling over. This was it. The endgame. He had reached his destination. All he had to do was find exactly where the missing piece was.

Chapter 11

It was a large area, and, if he was honest, he didn't really know where to start. He used to play a game called 'hotter or colder' when he was a lot younger, and he still played it occasionally with Josie, where, if he was getting closer to whatever he was looking for, someone would say 'hot', and, if he was moving away from it, someone would say 'cold'. He figured he needed to do the same thing now with the piece of the Globe he had in his pocket, a brighter glow indicating he would be moving closer to what he was searching for. What he didn't want, however, was for everyone else to think he was some kind of lunatic by spinning around in circles, so he cradled the piece in his hand and hid it from view, holding it close to his leg and only opening his hand every now and again to make sure he could see how the piece changed.

He walked towards the tower, regularly checking that the piece was, indeed, still glowing brightly. It was definitely becoming more intense, so he calculated that he must be going in the right direction. As he got nearer, he noticed a couple of armed soldiers walking around, so decided not to look too suspicious, waiting until their backs were turned before checking the piece he was holding again. Brighter still! He hadn't imagined it could get any brighter, but it was. He reached the foot of the tower, and saw a long line of people waiting to enter. He wasn't going to join the queue just yet, though, and wanted first to walk around the tower to see if it was hidden somewhere outside. It would have been a huge waste to walk up the two hundred and seventy-three steps, as he had seen advertised, if the piece was actually on the ground the whole time! He scoured the entire base of the tower, but couldn't see any sight of it. Noah was starting to get a tiny bit worried that in such a large space it would be simply impossible to locate a tiny, one-inch piece of a Globe that usually lived thousands of miles away in England. This seemed ridiculously absurd, and he was starting to lose all hope.

There was one more thing he could do, and that was to climb all those steps to get to the top of the tower. Surely he would be able to find it somewhere on his journey, even if it took him hours to do so. The site closed at ten pm, so he still had a good nine or ten hours to find what he needed. He checked the money in his pocket, and saw that he still had hundreds of euros left, enough to go up the tower about fifty times if needed.

He purchased a ticket from the office, and joined the back of the queue, glad he had thought to buy a small bottle of water as well. The midday heat was almost unbearable, so he took a big swig of water, wiping his mouth with his sleeve. The line was now moving quite quickly, however, and, before long, he had ducked his head and walked in through the wooden door.

He was surprised how dark it was in the tower, and also that it was hollow in the middle. There were spiral steps winding around the edge, and all the tourists followed one another in a long line, snaking up the stone staircase. Noah was constantly looking left and right for any sign of the piece, but didn't dare to take the other one out of his pocket to check, just in case it fell all the way to the bottom, forcing him to search for that as well!

It took the queue of sightseers fifteen minutes to walk all the way to the top, the line only moving as quickly as its slowest chain, which turned out to be a doddery Frenchman in his sixties. Noah was starting to get a bit anxious, but at least he was secure in the knowledge that he hadn't missed the piece on his way up.

They stopped climbing, and Noah stepped out to an area with a fantastic view all the way around the city. There were about forty people at the top of the tower, and there wasn't a lot of room to move, so he was careful where he stood. He found a corner with fewer people around, and carefully pulled the piece out of his pocket. It was shining as brightly as he had ever seen it, and as he walked around the top of the tower he monitored it, checking if he was getting 'hotter or colder'. Half-way around the tower, the piece was glowing so brightly that the light was almost visible through his closed fist. Noah looked around him to see if anyone was watching, which fortunately they weren't.

The piece safely returned to his pocket, he continued the search for its counterpart. He looked on the floor, under any loose stones, and on the inside wall. Nothing. No sign of it. He looked higher up in case it was trapped above his head. Nope, not there either. He was totally perplexed. The other piece indicated it was here, and yet he couldn't find any trace of it. He stood up and leaned over the side of the tower, and stared at the ground below, the tourists seeming like ants from his lofty position.

Something caught his eye – a reflection from a shiny object about fifty centimetres below where he was. He craned his neck to see if he could get a better view of what he hoped it was. He let out a short gasp when he saw exactly what it was – the piece he was looking for! Stuck to the outside of the tower. Yes, he thought, realising he had finally found it. The only problem, was that he couldn't reach it. How on earth was he going to get his hands on it, especially with this protective netting around the top of the tower?

He investigated a little more closely, and saw a small opening at the foot of the netting where it had been ripped. It wasn't particularly large, but it was probably big enough for him to fit his arm through. He took one final look around him, and saw that no-one was watching him, so knelt down and forced his arm through. He felt the netting rip a little more as he leant against it, trying to stretch his arm that little bit further to grab what he needed. He was so close, he could almost touch it, but just needed to reach a little… bit… more.

He heard another small tear in the netting, his adult body putting too much stress on the already worn safety barrier. His whole weight was now resting against it as he strained to touch the piece with his fingers. The fabric gave way a little more, and he was able to move a little bit closer to the piece until he could, at last, touch it. He had done it! He clasped his fingers around it, pulling it closer to him, until he was certain that he had full control of it.

He was partially hanging out of the mesh now, his head and shoulders more outside the tower than inside. Just at the moment when he was about to stand up, a crowd of tourists came past and knocked against him. He reached out to hold on to something, but it was too late, and he fell forward, head first, tumbling off the top of the Leaning Tower of Pisa!

Chapter 12

The floor was rushing towards him, a scared group of onlookers staring at him and screaming, pointing to others standing nearby. Quick as a flash, Noah reached into his pocket and pulled out the other piece of the Globe. He pushed both pieces against each other and immediately saw a bright light, and heard a snapping noise as if a giant whip had cracked through the air. A fraction of a second before he would have hit the floor, he felt himself gently falling onto the grassy patch in between the circle of the seven trees back in the World Wide Wood.

"Uumph," he grunted, as he rolled onto his front. He saw Mr Atlas strolling back from the row of trees from where Noah had started his adventure no more than twenty-four hours ago. Except for them, of course, it had only been a matter of seconds. Noah stood up, and could instantly tell he was no longer a man, but a boy of fourteen again.

"Noah, my boy. I take it from your arrival that you have been successful. Fun trip to Europe, was it? Tell me all about your adventure," he said, beaming from ear to ear. "Do you have the pieces, then?"

Noah laughed and laughed. And carried on laughing. He handed the two pieces over, and Mr Atlas hurried into the shop. The squirrels followed, and Noah brought up the rear, suddenly exhausted from his Italian exploits. He watched as Mr Atlas carefully lowered the Globe from the shelf, and the old man slotted the two pieces into their respective places, the Globe shining a tiny bit more intensely.

Mr Atlas looked at Noah more seriously. "What you have done today is truly remarkable, and I hope one day you will see exactly what all this means. I do want to hear about your adventures, but I fear you might have to go home straight away otherwise your mum will be worried. I can see from the piece that you went to Italy, but I just want to know how long you were there."

"It was about a day in total. I slept in a hotel in Florence and then found the piece on the Leaning Tower of Pisa."

"Marvelous, marvelous. Now, off you go, Noah. But listen, do you think you might want to come back tomorrow morning and see how else you can help with the World Wide Wood?"

"Absolutely!" Noah said with determination and glee. "I'll be here." He started to walk out of the shop, the bell giving the same little ring as he opened the door.

"Oh, and Noah."

"Yes," he said as he turned around.

"Don't forget the mayo!" Mr Atlas smiled, throwing him the squeezy bottle. Noah deftly caught it with one hand, and headed home.

Four minutes later, he was safely back in his own kitchen, and, smiling, he passed the bottle of mayonnaise to his mum.

"Blimey, Noah. You took your time, didn't you? Where did you go to buy this? London?"

Noah just walked up to his mum and gave her a massive hug. "You'd be surprised, mum. You'd be surprised," and he bounced upstairs, full of new found energy, before she had a chance to reply. He closed his bedroom door and collapsed on the bed.

"Wow. That was amazing! Maybe moving to this pokey little village might not be so bad after all," he said to himself with a huge grin on his face. "I can't wait to get back to the World Wide Wood and see what my next adventure might be!"

The End

Acknowledgements

First of all, thank you to my wife, Karen, for her constant support and encouragement, and for her unwavering belief in me and *The World Wide Wood* from day one.

Thank you to my children, Sullivan and Zoe, who have inspired my story-telling creativity over the years.

Thank you to Keith and Karolina at MTP for their knowledge, guidance and expertise during the publishing process.

And a massive thanks to my enthusiastic proofreaders, Summer, James and Josh, for their invaluable feedback.

About the Author

When he's not writing, Mike Rymarz spends his free time topping up his general knowledge, learning about the world, and dreaming about where he will travel to next.

Available worldwide from Amazon

——————————

www.mtp.agency

www.facebook.com/mtp.agency

@mtp_agency

Michael Terence
Publishing

Printed in Great Britain
by Amazon